The Adventures of Max and Lily

Pawan

 pencil

ISBN 978-93-5667-499-8
© Pawan 2023
Published in India 2023 by Pencil

A brand of
One Point Six Technologies Pvt. Ltd.
123, Building J2, Shram Seva Premises,
Wadala Truck Terminal, Wadala (E)
Mumbai 400037, Maharashtra, INDIA
E connect@thepencilapp.com
W www.thepencilapp.com

Author biography

The author of this book has a diverse background in writing, including experience writing blogs, business articles, and management lessons. However, his passion for storytelling and love of children has led them to venture into writing children's books.

As someone who loves kids, the author is dedicated to adding value to their lives through his writing. He understands the power of storytelling in shaping young minds and inspiring a sense of wonder and curiosity about the world. Through his work, he hopes to instill important values such as teamwork, courage, and kindness in young readers.

His experience of writing articles, blogs and management lessons has given him a strong foundation, which he has used to develop the plot and themes of this book. He approaches each chapter with a clear understanding of the lessons he want to impart, while also keeping in mind the need for engaging characters and an exciting plot to keep young readers interested.

Despite his success in writing for a business audience, the author understands that writing for children requires a different set of skills and sensibilities. He has worked hard to adapt his writing style to create a book that is both entertaining and educational for young readers.

CONTENTS

Foreword

Dear young readers,

It is with great pleasure that I introduce this book to you, which is filled with exciting adventures and magical moments. As a writer, it brings me immense joy to create stories that not only entertain but also inspire young minds.

The characters in this book, Max and Lily, go on an unforgettable journey, discovering new things and experiencing various emotions along the way. Through their adventures, they learn valuable lessons about friendship, teamwork, courage, and perseverance.

As a parent, I understand how important it is to find books that not only engage children but also provide them with valuable insights into life. Therefore, I have written this book with the hope of igniting the imagination and curiosity of young readers and inspiring them to embark on their own adventures.

I encourage you to join Max and Lily on their journey and let your imagination run wild. Perhaps you will discover your own treasure map or magical garden along the way.

Happy reading!

Best regards

Pawan

Acknowledgements

I would like to express our heartfelt gratitude to my 9year old daughter HIYA who through her currosity and imagination has contributed to the making of this book.
I also extend our sincere thanks to my family and friends for their constant support and encouragement throughout this journey.

I would also like to express our gratitude to the publishing team for their tireless efforts in making this book a reality.

Lastly, I would like to thank all my young readers for choosing this book and hope that it sparks joy, wonder and a love for storytelling in you.

Thank you all!

Chapter 1 The Mysterious Treasure Map

Max and Lily were playing in their backyard on a sunny day. Max was trying to catch a butterfly while Lily was reading a book under a tree. Suddenly, Max stumbled upon something hard buried in the soil. He started digging around it and soon found a small, rusty box.

Excitedly, Max and Lily opened the box and found an old piece of paper inside. It was a map that showed the way to a mysterious treasure hidden in a far-off land.

Max and Lily were thrilled at the prospect of going on a treasure hunt. They ran to their mom to show her the map and begged her to take them on an adventure to find the treasure. Their mom, who was always up for a good adventure, agreed to take them on the treasure hunt.

They quickly packed their bags with snacks, water, and some essential supplies for the trip. They also took their bicycles as they planned to travel long distances on their journey.

As they set off on their adventure, they studied the map carefully. The map showed them a path through the jungle, across a river, over the mountains, and finally to a remote island.

Max and Lily were excited about the journey, but they knew it wouldn't be easy. They would have to face many challenges and obstacles on their way, but they were determined to find the treasure.

As they cycled through the jungle, they faced many difficulties. The path was rocky, and they had to cross several streams and climb steep hills. They were tired and hungry, but they didn't give up.

After a few hours, they finally made it through the jungle and reached the river. They looked around for a boat, but there was none. They had to figure out how to cross the river to continue their journey.

Lily remembered reading in her book about a simple technique to build a raft. They collected wood and ropes and built a small raft. They got on the raft and used a stick to guide it across the river.

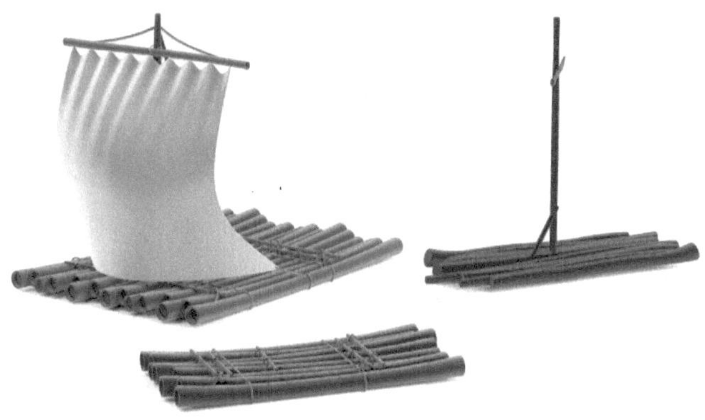

As they reached the other side, they saw a beautiful mountain range ahead of them. They knew they had to cross the mountains to reach the remote island where the treasure was hidden.

Max and Lily cycled up the steep mountain, and it was the toughest part of their journey. The air was thin, and they were panting, but they didn't give up. They were determined to reach the top of the mountain and find the treasure.

As they reached the summit, they saw a beautiful island ahead of them. The island was covered with lush green trees and surrounded by clear blue water.
They knew the treasure was somewhere on the island, and they were excited to explore it.

But as they started their descent, they saw a spooky, abandoned house on the island. The house looked haunted, and they were scared to go near it. However, the map indicated that the treasure was inside the house.

Max and Lily decided to summon their courage and explore the house. They entered the house and found a secret room hidden behind a bookshelf. Inside the room, they found a chest full of gold coins and precious jewels.

Max and Lily couldn't believe their luck. They had found the treasure, and it was more than they had ever imagined. They hugged each other and jumped with joy.

As they cycled back home, they knew they had gone on an unforgettable adventure. They had overcome challenges, explored new places, and found treasure. They knew that they would always treasure this memory and look forward to their next adventure.

Chapter 2 Lost in the Jungle

Max and Lily had been wandering through the jungle for hours, hoping to find their way back to civilization. The sun was starting to set and they were getting tired, hungry and thirsty. Max's stomach was growling, and Lily's feet were aching. They were lost and there was no sign of anyone or anything around them.

Lily looked around nervously, feeling a sense of unease. The dense jungle was filled with unfamiliar sounds and creatures she had never seen before. The rustling of leaves and the chirping of birds echoed around them, making it difficult for them to hear each other. Max tried to reassure her, telling her that they would find their way out soon enough.

But soon, the sun had set and it was getting darker by the minute. Max decided to climb up a tall tree to see if he could spot any signs of civilization. Lily was hesitant at first, but Max convinced her that it was the only way to find their way back.

Max climbed up the tree, careful not to slip on the rough bark. When he reached the top, he looked around, hoping to see something that would guide them to safety. But all he saw was more jungle - trees, vines, and thick foliage.

As Max was looking around, he spotted a faint light in the distance. He was sure that it was not the sun, and that it was coming from some sort of man-made structure. Max climbed down the tree and excitedly told Lily what he had seen.

Lily was hesitant to follow Max in the direction of the light, but Max convinced her that it was their only hope of finding their way back to civilization. They walked towards the light, using a small flashlight that Max had brought with him. They were careful not to trip on the vines or step on any dangerous animals that might be lurking in the darkness.

After walking for what seemed like hours, Max and Lily finally reached the source of the light. It was a small hut made of branches and leaves. There was smoke coming out of the chimney, indicating that someone was inside. Max and Lily looked at each other nervously, wondering who could be living in such a remote area. Max decided to knock on the door, hoping that whoever was inside would be able to help them.

A tall, muscular man with a thick beard and sharp eyes opened the door. He looked at Max and Lily suspiciously, asking them who they were and what they were doing there. Max explained that they were lost and were looking for a way back to civilization. The man listened to Max's explanation and then invited them inside. He introduced himself as Jack, a retired hunter who lived in the jungle. He had lived there for years and knew the area like the back of his hand.

Jack offered Max and Lily some food and water, which they gratefully accepted. Max explained that they had been searching for civilization, but had lost their way. Jack listened carefully and then told them that the only way to find their way back was to follow a river that flowed through the jungle.

Jack gave Max and Lily a map of the area, which showed the location of the river. He also gave them a compass and some advice on how to navigate through the jungle safely. Max and Lily thanked Jack for his help and then set off towards the river.

After walking for what seemed like hours, Max and Lily finally reached the river. They followed the river downstream, hoping that it would lead them to civilization. They were tired and hungry, but they did not give up.

Finally, after walking for several more hours, Max and Lily saw a small village in the distance. They were overjoyed and ran towards the village, hoping to find help. As they entered the village, they were greeted by friendly faces and warm smiles

Chapter 3 The Treasure Hunt

After their dangerous journey through the jungle, Max and Lily finally arrived at the spot marked on the treasure map. The sun was setting, and they knew they had to find the treasure quickly. They started digging with their shovels, and soon enough, they found a small wooden chest buried in the ground.

Excitedly, they opened the chest and found it filled with gold coins, shiny jewels, and precious artifacts. Max and Lily couldn't believe their eyes, they had found a real treasure! But as they started to examine the contents of the chest, they realized that there was something missing.

*"The diamond!"*Max exclaimed. *"The biggest diamond in the world, it's not here!"*

The map had promised the biggest diamond in the world, and yet it was nowhere to be found. Max and Lily were disappointed, but they knew they had to keep searching.

They started exploring the area around them, searching for any clues that could lead them to the missing diamond. As they walked, they heard a faint sound coming from a nearby cave. Curious, they followed the sound and entered the cave. Inside, they found an old, worn-out map.

Max and Lily carefully examined the map and realized that it was a map to a hidden temple in the mountains. The temple was said to contain the biggest diamond in the world. Excited about their new discovery, Max and Lily knew they had to set out for the mountains immediately. They packed their bags and started their journey, determined to find the missing diamond.

The journey was long and difficult. The mountains were steep, and the weather was harsh. But Max and Lily didn't give up. They were determined to find the diamond and complete their treasure hunt.

Finally, after many days of walking, they reached the hidden temple. The temple was covered in vines and surrounded by a moat. Max and Lily looked at each other, wondering how they were going to get inside.

Suddenly, they heard a voice behind them. *"Looking for something?"* It was an old man who looked like he had been living in the temple for years.

Max and Lily explained their quest to the old man, and he offered to help them get inside the temple. He showed them a secret entrance and led them inside.

The temple was dark and eerie, and Max and Lily felt like they were in a movie. They carefully made their way through the maze-like corridors, avoiding traps and obstacles along the way.

Finally, they reached the room where the diamond was supposed to be kept. But when they entered the room, they found it empty. The diamond was gone.

Max and Lily were disappointed, but they didn't give up. They searched the room for any clues and found a small piece of paper. The paper had a strange symbol on it that Max and Lily had never seen before.

They showed the symbol to the old man, who gasped in surprise. *"This symbol belongs to the legendary Diamond Thief,"* he said. *"He's been stealing the world's biggest diamonds for years. If anyone can help you find the missing diamond, it's him."*

Max and Lily knew they had to find the Diamond Thief. They left the temple and started their journey to track down the thief and retrieve the diamond.

As they walked, they knew that their journey wasn't over yet. But Max and Lily were determined to find the diamond and complete their treasure hunt. They had come too far to give up now.

Chapter 4 The Haunted House

As Max and Lily travelled from the temple, there was no sign of the treasure or the haunted house. All they could see was the dense forest surrounding them.
Lily shuddered at the thought of spending the night in the jungle. Max could see the fear in her eyes and knew he had to do something to cheer her up. "*Hey, look at the bright side,*" he said, "*at least we have each other.*"

Lily smiled weakly, but Max knew he had to come up with a better plan. "Let's set up camp here for the night," he said, "and start our treasure hunt again in the morning."

They quickly gathered some twigs and branches and made a small fire. Max rummaged through his backpack and found some snacks and water. They sat around the fire, munching on their food, and talking about their adventure so far.

As the night grew darker, the forest seemed to come alive with strange sounds. Max and Lily could hear the rustling of leaves, the hooting of an owl, and the distant howl of a wolf. Lily huddled closer to Max, feeling scared.

Suddenly, they heard a loud creaking noise, and the ground shook beneath their feet. Max and Lily jumped up, looking around for the source of the sound. That's when they saw it – a huge, dilapidated mansion in the distance. It was the haunted house they had been looking for.

Max could feel his heart racing with excitement. This was their chance to find the treasure. "*Let's go,*" he said, grabbing Lily's hand, "*we have a haunted house to explore.*"

Max and Lily made their way through the haunted house, carefully searching every room for any clues that might lead them to the treasure. The dusty old furniture and creaky floorboards made eerie noises as they tiptoed around, making the whole place feel like it was alive.

As they were searching through an old study, Max suddenly heard a strange noise coming from behind a bookshelf. Curious, he pushed the shelf aside and revealed a hidden door.

Lily gasped as Max stepped through the door, and they found themselves in a small, dimly lit room. In the center of the room was a table with a large, glowing diamond resting on it. Max and Lily stared in awe, unable to believe their luck.

But their joy was short-lived, as suddenly the door slammed shut behind them, and they heard footsteps approaching. Max and Lily turned to see the masked man they had encountered earlier, a look of greed in his eyes.
"*You found my diamond,*" he growled, his voice cold and menacing. "*I've been looking for that for a long time. Hand it over.*"

Max and Lily hesitated, but the man was already lunging towards them. Max quickly grabbed the diamond and shoved it into his backpack, hoping to keep it safe. The thief was furious and began chasing Max and Lily around the room, determined to get his hands on the diamond. Max and Lily ran as fast as they could, trying to dodge the thief's grasp.

Finally, they managed to dodge past the thief and make it to the door. But just as they were about to escape, the thief caught up to them and grabbed Lily by the arm.

Max was terrified, unsure of what to do. But then he remembered the flashlight in his backpack and quickly shined it in the thief's face, blinding him and causing him to let go of Lily.

With a burst of energy, Max and Lily sprinted out of the haunted house and into the night, their hearts pounding with adrenaline. As they caught their breath, they looked at each other, both realizing that they had narrowly escaped a dangerous situation.

But despite the danger, they had also managed to find the diamond, and it was all thanks to their courage and quick thinking. As they made their way back home, they couldn't help but feel a sense of pride and accomplishment. They had just had their first real adventure, and it was something they would never forget.

Chapter 5 The Magical Garden

After escaping the haunted house, Max and Lily were relieved to be outside in the fresh air once again. They looked around and found themselves in a beautiful garden filled with colorful flowers, fragrant herbs, and tall trees. It was unlike any garden they had ever seen before.

As they walked around, they noticed that the flowers and plants seemed to be glowing and sparkling in the sunlight. The air was filled with the sweet scent of lavender, and the sound of birds singing could be heard in the distance.

*"This garden is magical,"*said Lily, her eyes wide with wonder.

Max nodded in agreement. *"I wonder who takes care of this place. It's so beautiful."*

Just then, they heard a rustling sound in the bushes. They turned to see a small fairy with delicate wings and a dress made of flower petals. She had a kind smile on her face. "*Greetings, travelers,*" she said in a soft voice. "*Welcome to the magical garden. I am the fairy guardian of this place.*"

Max and Lily were surprised but excited to meet a fairy. They introduced themselves and told the fairy about their adventure so far.

The fairy listened intently and then said, "*You are very brave to have come this far. I have been watching you, and I know that you are on a quest to find the treasure. The treasure you seek is not just any treasure, but a magical one that can bring joy and happiness to everyone who possesses it.*"

Max and Lily were intrigued. "*But how do we find the treasure?*" asked Lily.

The fairy smiled. *"The treasure is hidden deep within the garden, but it is not easy to find. You must follow the clues that I will give you, and only then will you be able to discover the treasure."*

The fairy then handed them a piece of paper with a riddle written on it.

"In the garden, where the roses bloom, Find the statue, and look at its plume. It will point the way to your next clue, And lead you closer to your treasure true."

Max and Lily looked at each other, feeling excited and a little nervous. They knew that the treasure was close, but also that they had to solve the riddles and clues to find it.

They thanked the fairy and set off to explore the garden. They followed the path and soon came across a beautiful statue of a swan with a plume on its head.

As they looked at the plume, they noticed that it was pointing towards a nearby flower bed.

They hurried over to the flower bed and saw a small box hidden among the flowers. Inside the box was another clue, written on a piece of parchment.

"From the flower bed, take a left, And cross the bridge, but do not rest. The pond is where your next clue lies, Beneath the lilies, it will surprise."

Max and Lily followed the instructions and soon arrived at a small pond filled with lilies. They searched under the lilies and found a small key hidden there. The key looked old and rusted, but they knew it was important.

The fairy appeared again, *"Well done, young adventurers. You have solved the second clue. But beware, the diamond thief you encountered earlier is also after the treasure. You must be careful."*

Max and Lily nodded, feeling determined to find the treasure and keep it out of the hands of the diamond thief.

They continued their journey, following the clues and overcoming obstacles along the way. As they got closer to the treasure, the clues became more challenging, but they never gave up.

Finally, they arrived at the heart of the garden, where a large tree with twisted branches stood. As they approached the tree, they saw a small opening at its base. They used the key to unlock the opening and found

Chapter 6 The Amazing Circus

Max and Lily were having the time of their lives exploring the magical garden. They saw all sorts of exotic plants and animals, and even got to ride on the back of a friendly unicorn! Eventually, though, it was time to move on to their next adventure: visiting the circus.

The circus was set up in a big field just outside of town, and as soon as Max and Lily arrived, they could hear the sound of music and laughter in the air. They made their way through the crowds of people and found a good spot to watch the show.

The first act was a group of acrobats who performed amazing feats of strength and balance high up in the air.

Max and Lily were both on the edge of their seats, watching as the acrobats flipped and twisted through the air. They even gasped as one of the performers shot out of a cannon and flew through a ring of fire!

Next up was a group of clowns who had everyone in the audience laughing and cheering. One clown even pulled Max up on stage to be part of the act! Max was nervous at first, but soon found himself laughing and having fun with the silly clowns.

After the clowns, it was time for the animal acts. Max and Lily were a bit nervous about this part, as they had heard stories about circuses being cruel to animals. But as soon as they saw the trainers interacting with their animals, they could tell that these animals were loved and well taken care of.

There were tigers who jumped through fiery hoops, elephants who balanced on giant balls, and even a group of dogs who did tricks with frisbees. Max and Lily were amazed at how intelligent and talented these animals were.

Finally, it was time for the grand finale. A group of performers came out with huge colorful wings on their backs and began to dance and twirl through the air. Max and Lily could hardly believe their eyes as the performers soared higher and higher, spinning and flipping through the air with grace and precision.

As the show came to an end, Max and Lily clapped and cheered with the rest of the audience. They had never seen anything like the amazing circus before!

As they walked back to their car, Max turned to Lily and said, "This has been the best adventure yet!"
Lily smiled and replied, "*I can't wait to see what our next adventure will be!*"

Chapter 7 The Space Adventure

Max and Lily had just finished their incredible visit to the circus, and now they were ready for their next adventure. They sat down together, and Max pulled out the map to see what their next destination would be.

*'Whoa! It looks like our next adventure is going to be out of this world,'*exclaimed Lily.

Max looked at the map closely, and sure enough, the next clue led them to a space center. He was amazed, but he couldn't wait to see what it was like.

They hopped into their car and drove to the space center. The building was enormous, and they could see rockets on display outside. They ran towards the entrance, eager to explore the mysteries of space.

Once inside, they saw many amazing things, including a real astronaut suit and a lunar module. They also learned a lot about the planets in our solar system and the constellations in the night sky.

Max and Lily were both fascinated, but then something caught their eye - a spaceship simulator! They couldn't resist trying it out. The simulator was designed to feel like a real spaceship, and they felt like they were really in space.

They even got to practice docking the spaceship with the International Space Station.

After the simulator, they explored more exhibits and learned about the history of space travel. They saw a replica of the first rocket to land on the moon, and they were amazed by how small it was. They also saw a spacesuit that was worn by a real astronaut on a mission.

As they were about to leave, they stumbled upon a scientist who was looking for volunteers to help with an experiment. Max and Lily jumped at the opportunity to help out.

The experiment involved creating a model of the solar system using different sizes of balls and lights to represent the planets and the sun. Max and Lily learned a lot about the relative distances between planets and the scale of the solar system. They were amazed at how tiny Earth was compared to some of the other planets.

As they were leaving the space center, Max and Lily couldn't stop talking about all the amazing things they had seen and learned. They both agreed that it was one of the best adventures they had ever had.

On their drive home, Max and Lily noticed that the sky was full of stars. They both smiled, knowing that they had just explored a small part of the vast universe. They both knew that they wanted to explore more and more, and who knows where their next adventure might take them.

Chapter 8 The Underwater World

Max and Lily had finally returned after their thrilling space adventure. They had seen the beauty of the stars and the vastness of the universe, but now they were ready for a new adventure. Lily had heard about an underwater world where fish swam in rainbow colors, and Max was eager to explore it.

They gathered their gear and headed to the coast, where they met Captain Jack, a grizzled old sailor with a weathered face and a peg leg. He welcomed them aboard his boat, The Sea Dragon, and they set sail for the underwater world.

As they journeyed out to sea, Max and Lily marveled at the vastness of the ocean. They saw dolphins leaping out of the water and whales spouting water into the air. The Sea Dragon cut through the waves, leaving a trail of frothy white foam in its wake.

After several hours of sailing, they finally reached their destination. The water was crystal clear, and they could see fish swimming just below the surface. Captain Jack donned his scuba gear and led Max and Lily into the water.

As they descended, Max and Lily felt their ears pop from the pressure. But soon, they were surrounded by a whole new world. Fish of every color and shape swam around them, and they saw giant clams with iridescent shells and sea anemones waving their tentacles in the current.

They swam deeper and saw a shipwreck on the ocean floor. It was covered in coral and teeming with fish. Max swam inside and saw a treasure chest. He opened it and found a beautiful pearl necklace.

But suddenly, they heard a loud noise. They turned to see a giant octopus emerging from a nearby cave. Its tentacles were as thick as tree trunks, and its eyes glowed with an eerie light. The octopus lashed out at them, but Captain Jack was ready. He pulled out a flare and waved it in front of the octopus. The creature recoiled in fear and retreated back into the cave.

Max, Lily, and Captain Jack continued their underwater adventure, seeing schools of fish darting around them and sea turtles gliding gracefully through the water. They even saw a shark, but it didn't seem interested in them and swam off into the distance.

As they swam back up to the surface, Max and Lily couldn't stop talking about everything they had seen. They thanked Captain Jack for the amazing adventure and promised to come back someday.

Back on land, Max and Lily were still filled with wonder at the amazing world they had discovered. They knew that there were many more adventures waiting for them in the future, and they couldn't wait to explore them all.

Epilogue Max and Lily's Next Adventure

As Max and Lily returned from their thrilling space adventure, they were amazed at how much they had learned and experienced on their treasure-hunting journey. They had faced challenges, solved puzzles, and made new friends along the way.

Back at home, they shared their stories with their parents and friends, and even presented a slideshow of their adventure. Everyone was amazed and impressed by the children's bravery and intelligence.

Max and Lily knew that their treasure hunt was just the beginning of their adventures. They were eager to explore more of the world and learn about new places, cultures, and people.

Inspired by their journey, Max and Lily decided to start their own treasure-hunting club for kids in their neighborhood. They invited other children to join them on their adventures and learn about the world around them.

The club quickly became popular, and soon Max and Lily found themselves leading a group of enthusiastic treasure hunters on exciting journeys. They discovered new treasures, solved mysteries, and made lasting memories.

As they grew older, Max and Lily remained close friends and continued to explore the world together. They even wrote a book about their adventures, hoping to inspire other children to follow in their footsteps and discover the wonders of the world around them.

And so, Max and Lily's treasure-hunting adventures came full circle. What had started as a simple game of hide-and-seek led them on a journey of a lifetime, filled with excitement, wonder, and discovery.

They knew that their adventures were just the beginning, and they were excited to see where their next journey would take them.